CLASS PRESIDENT

By Johanna Hurwitz

The Adventures of Ali Baba Bernstein
Aldo Applesauce
Aldo Ice Cream
Aldo Peanut Butter
Baseball Fever
Busybody Nora
Class Clown
Class President
The Cold and Hot Winter
DeDe Takes Charge!
"E" Is for Elisa
The Hot and Cold Summer
Hurray for Ali Baba Bernstein
Hurricane Elaine
The Law of Gravity
Much Ado About Aldo
New Neighbors for Nora
Nora and Mrs. Mind-Your-Own-Business
Once I Was a Plum Tree
The Rabbi's Girls
Rip-Roaring Russell
Russell and Elisa
Russell Rides Again
Russell Sprouts
School's Out
Superduper Teddy
Teacher's Pet
Tough-Luck Karen
Yellow Blue Jay

Johanna Hurwitz

CLASS PRESIDENT

Illustrated by Sheila Hamanaka

Morrow Junior Books · New York

Text copyright © 1990 by Johanna Hurwitz
Illustrations copyright © 1990 by Sheila Hamanaka
All rights reserved.
No part of this book may be reproduced
or utilized in any form or by any means,
electronic or mechanical, including photocopying,
recording or by any information storage and retrieval system,
without permission in writing from the Publisher.
Inquiries should be addressed to
William Morrow and Company, Inc.,
1350 Avenue of the Americas,
New York, NY 10019.
Printed in the United States of America.
3 4 5 6 7 8 9 10
Library of Congress Cataloging-in-Publication Data
Hurwitz, Johanna.
Class president / Johanna Hurwitz : illustrations by Sheila
Hamanaka.
p.   cm.
Summary: Julio hides his own leadership ambitions to help another
candidate in the election for class president.
ISBN 0-688-09114-8
[1. Elections—Fiction.   2. Schools—Fiction.   3. Hispanic
Americans—Fiction.]   I. Hamanaka, Sheila, ill.   II. Title.
PZ7.H9574Cm   1990
[Fic]—dc20   89-28600   CIP   AC

To Delia and Bill Gottlieb
They get my vote every time!

★ ★
CONTENTS

★1★
WHO
IS WHO-LIO?

Julio Sanchez ran all the way to school. He wouldn't have admitted it to anyone, but he was looking forward to the first day of fifth grade. He liked being in a roomful of kids. It was too bad that going to school also meant stuff like spending time on arithmetic and social studies.

The summer had been long and hot and boring. Julio had missed his school friends. He wondered if any of them had missed him. He wished he had been old enough to get a summer job like his brothers, Ramon and Nelson. With his mother and brothers off at work, he had stayed at home with his grandmother watching TV reruns. His grandmother had arthritis and couldn't help out much in the kitchen, so Julio had to make his own lunch almost every day.

Although he didn't like arithmetic, Julio had added up all his lunches in July and August. He had emptied a total of 17 jars of peanut butter onto 248 slices of bread to make 124 sandwiches. Gross!

Julio liked the variety of school lunches—but he wouldn't have admitted that, either. Everyone was supposed to hate school lunches, or at least, as Julio did, pretend to hate them.

A Safety Patrol monitor was stationed at the corner across the street from the school. Both Ramon and Nelson had been members of the Safety Patrol, and Julio looked forward to sixth grade when he, too, could wear the Safety Patrol blue sash with a silver badge pinned to it.

Julio patted the top of his head as he reached the school yard. His hair had been cut into spikes, just like his older brother Nelson's. The spikes kept falling down. Still, Julio hoped his new haircut would help him stand out in a special way.

The school yard was filled with kids. No one was ever late on the first day of school. It didn't take Julio long to find his classmates. Lucas Cott, Arthur Lewis, Sara Jane Cushman, Cricket Kaufman, and Zoe Mitchell were all standing in a group and talking.

"Hi. Give me five!" Julio called, raising his hand to slap a greeting with Lucas. The two boys were old pals even though they hardly had seen each other all summer. Lucas had gone to sleep-away camp for a month and then his family had taken a trip together.

Lucas slapped hands with Julio. "Have you heard the news?" he asked.

"I just got here," said Julio.

"Mrs. Upchurch is gone," said Cricket before Lucas could say anything.

They had all been promoted to Mrs. Upchurch's class on the last day of fourth grade.

"You mean old Upchuck isn't going to be our teacher?" asked Julio.

"How do you know she's not here?" asked Sara Jane Cushman. "None of the teachers is out in the yard yet. Only kids are waiting outside."

"I heard two teachers talking," said Cricket.

"One said, 'I'll miss Shirley,' and the other one said, 'It's too bad we didn't give a party for her in June.' Mrs. Upchurch's name was Shirley, so that proves she's the one they were talking about."

"Maybe she got a better job," said Lucas.

"Anything would be better than being here," said Julio, pretending to hate school.

Before there was time to talk any more about what Cricket had overheard, a bell rang. It was the signal to line up. Because it was the first day of school, everyone obeyed instantly. By tomorrow, they would all be less eager to enter the building. The excitement of the first day always wore off quickly.

Sixth-grade monitors showed the younger children where they were supposed to line up. The fifth graders didn't need Safety Patrol monitors. Next year, *they* would be wearing the blue sashes and giving the orders. Not every fifth grader dreamed of becoming a monitor, but Julio had wanted to be one even before he'd entered kindergarten, when Nelson had been a school monitor.

The second bell rang. The monitors directed

the lines of students to enter the building in alphabetical order by teacher. Mrs. Gordon's and Mrs. Hershey's fifth-grade classes entered the building, followed by Mrs. Upchurch's class.

It would be funny if she was there after all, Julio thought. But Mrs. Upchurch was not in her classroom. In her place was someone they had never seen before. It was a man. A man for a teacher! The only other men in the building were Mr. Herbertson, the principal, and Mr. Conners, the janitor. Julio hoped the teacher didn't turn out to be like old Herbertson, or they would be in real trouble.

"Good morning," the new teacher said. "I'm Ernesto Flores, your teacher for fifth grade."

In all his years in school, Julio had never heard a teacher tell her first name. Of course, the students always found out who they were—Joyce Hockaday, Augusta Schraalenburgh, Shirley Upchurch—but it was up to the students to discover this information for themselves. The new teacher had spoiled the game.

"Now I'd like to find out who you are," said Mr. Flores. He began to call the roll, starting with the boys.

Julio shook his head. Teachers *always* began with the girls.

"Julio Sanchez," called Mr. Flores, pronouncing it Hulio. That was the correct way to say the name in Spanish.

Several kids laughed. They had never heard Julio's name pronounced without the *J*.

Mr. Flores looked up from the roll book. "Isn't that how you say your name?" he asked Julio. "Or do you prefer Julio with a *J*?"

Julio shrugged his shoulders. "At home, they call me Hulio. But at school everyone calls me Julio."

"How do you feel about that?" asked the teacher. "Do you like two pronunciations of your name? It's a good Spanish name and you should be proud of it."

Julio grinned at his teacher. "I know," he said, "but it doesn't matter to me."

"Are you sure?" asked Mr. Flores. "Your name is a very important part of you."

Julio thought for a moment. "Okay," he said. "From now on, everyone call me Hulio."

Mr. Flores smiled. "Who-lio is who you are," he said. And everyone laughed.

When Mr. Flores reached the girls, Zoe raised her hand. "My name is pronounced Zo-eee even though it's spelled Z-O-E," she said. She didn't want the new teacher to make a mistake on her name, too.

After roll call, Mr. Flores told the class some of the things they would be studying. Julio noticed that everyone was on their very best behavior. No one called out or popped rubber bands or chewed gum.

In social studies, they were going to learn about the Spanish, French, Dutch, and English colonies.

"Puerto Rico, where I was born, used to be a Spanish colony," said Julio, raising his hand instead of calling out as he sometimes did.

"That's right," said Mr. Flores. "When we get to that, you can tell us about your memories of Puerto Rico."

Julio shook his head. "I came here when I was only eight months old. I don't remember anything."

Everyone laughed at that.

"Then you can interview your parents instead," Mr. Flores said.

Julio nodded. He didn't bother to explain that his father was no longer alive. He could interview his mother and grandmother. Maybe Ramon and Nelson could help him, too. It would be fun to learn more about the place where he had been born.

Julio had to admit that Mr. Flores had some interesting ideas. They were going to write their own books and publish them in the classroom. In arithmetic, they were each going to spend a million dollars before the month was over.

Julio let out a loud whistle. "A million dollars. Man, that's a lot of money."

"Yes it is," said the teacher. "It won't be easy to do."

There was a murmur of voices throughout the classroom. Everyone leaned over and started telling whoever sat next to them how they would spend a million dollars.

"Quiet down now," said Mr. Flores. "You'll have plenty of time to try to spend your money. Keep your plans to yourself for the time being."

The biggest news of all was that they were going to have an election for class president.

Julio sat up in his seat. He knew that the students elected class leaders in high school. He had heard his brothers talking about it, but he had never heard about an election in fifth grade. For one moment, he tried to imagine himself as class president, but he knew it could never happen. He was not special enough. Who would vote for him?

"Can we do it now?" asked Cricket.

Julio knew why Cricket was so eager for the class election. She was sure she would win.

"I don't think it's such a good idea to elect a president on the first day of school. Let's wait a couple of weeks until you all know each other better," said Mr. Flores.

Julio laughed to himself. He knew every single kid in the room. Some of them he had known since kindergarten. Arthur Lewis had glasses with different frames from the ones he had worn last year. Cricket Kaufman had gotten her hair cut over the summer. Sara Jane Cushman had come back to school wearing braces on her teeth. Otherwise, they were all the same.

The only one who didn't know the students yet was Mr. Flores, and he wouldn't even be voting. On the other hand, Julio was in no hurry to see Cricket become class president. Since there was no chance for him, he would try to get Lucas to run against Cricket.

By eleven o'clock, Julio was already hungry. By lunchtime, he was starving. He had studied the September menu that Mr. Flores had given out to the class. Today, on the first day of school, they were serving his all-time favorite—big squares of pizza with pepperoni, tossed salad, and cherry Jell-O with topping.

Mr. Flores's students sat together to talk about their first morning in fifth grade.

"What do you think of Mr. Flores, Hulio?" asked Lucas.

"How's that cherry *H*ell-O you're eating?" asked Cricket.

"How's your apple *h*uice, Sara *H*ane?" asked Zoe.

Everyone began thinking of *j* words that they could alter to a Spanish pronunciation. Julio took the teasing good-naturedly. Some kids would probably be crying by now, he thought. To him, it was all a joke, or a *h*oke if you changed the *j* to an *h*.

Everyone was so busy thinking up *j* words that they forgot about the class election. They even forgot to discuss their new teacher. He was probably going to turn out to be just like the old teachers, anyway. Old or new, men or women, teachers were teachers.

★2★
LUCAS
FOR PRESIDENT?

When the students were dismissed at three o'clock, Julio walked partway home with Lucas.

"Cricket wants to run for class president," Julio said.

"She also wants to run for President of the United States," Lucas said.

Both boys laughed. Cricket had told everyone that she wanted to be the first woman President. She had been talking about it since third grade.

Julio wished that Lucas would say, "Julio, you

would make a great president," but Lucas didn't say anything.

Finally, Julio said, "I think *you* should run."

"Me? I don't want to be President of the United States," said Lucas. "I want to be the baseball commissioner. Then I could go to all the games for free."

"I don't mean President of the United States," said Julio. "I meant you should run against Cricket. You'd make a good president for our class."

Lucas shrugged.

"I'll help you campaign," Julio promised. "I'll tell everyone to vote for you."

"I'll think about it," said Lucas.

"Great," said Julio.

If he couldn't be class president himself, he would rather have his best friend elected instead of Cricket.

They came to the street where they each went in a different direction. When Julio got home, he could hear the television even before he opened the door. His grandmother was a little deaf and she always turned the volume way up when she was watching a soap opera.

Julio greeted her in Spanish. He only knew a little Spanish, although he could understand the language when his mother and grandmother spoke together. Now his grandmother gestured for him to be quiet. Something important was happening on the screen. A man was kissing a woman and whispering something in her ear. Gross!

For homework, Mr. Flores had told everyone to bring in magazines and mail-order catalogs. "Then you can plan how you are going to spend your million dollars," he had said.

Julio's mother didn't get any mail-order catalogs, but he could always take magazines to school. His mother was head chambermaid at the Sycamore Shade Motor Inn. If she found something discarded in a room she was cleaning, she was permitted to take it home. Mrs. Sanchez was always bringing home magazines and half-empty boxes of candy and fruit.

Julio's grandmother couldn't read English but she liked to look at the pictures in the magazines. Julio rarely looked at the magazines himself, except when his grandmother called his attention to a picture of a fancy house or an elegant bedroom that looked fit only for a princess or a movie star.

That afternoon, Julio looked through a stack of magazines. There were advertisements for the latest models of several cars. With his pretend million dollars, Julio decided he would buy one for his mother. It was true that she didn't know how to drive, but Ramon could teach her. He would buy Ramon a new car, too. Ramon's car was so old that it ran some days and some days it didn't. Then he decided that he should buy Nelson a car, too. Julio liked to be fair.

When Nelson came in from high school, Julio was still turning the glossy pages.

"I get to spend a million dollars in arithmetic," Julio told his brother.

"Come off it," said Nelson.

"It's just for arithmetic," Julio explained. "We've got a new teacher, Mr. Flores. And he told us to make a list of all the things we want to buy and add up the prices. I'm going to buy you a car. What color do you want?"

Nelson laughed. "Wait till I tell the guys in my driver's-ed class about that!"

"Well, I would if I had a real million dollars," said Julio.

"Thanks," Nelson said. "If I had a million dollars, I'd buy you one, too, even though you wouldn't be allowed to drive it until you were sixteen." He thought for a moment. "Spending fake money isn't what I did in fifth grade," he said. "Aren't you going to do any fractions? Fifth grade is supposed to be fractions."

Julio shrugged. "Maybe we'll do fractions next," he said. He hoped Mr. Flores knew what he was doing. Maybe he was so new at teaching that he was going to teach them all the wrong things.

At supper, Mrs. Sanchez wanted to know all about Julio's first day at school.

"I have a new teacher," he said. "His name is Ernesto Flores."

"You see," Mrs. Sanchez said, turning to Ramon. "You could be a teacher, too."

"We'll see, Mom," Ramon said. "This is just my first semester of college. I'm not sure what I want to study yet."

Julio knew his mother was very proud that

Ramon was taking courses at a junior college. She always made sure her sons did their home- work and studied for exams.

"We're going to have a class election," Julio said. "Cricket wants to be class president. I think Lucas should run against her."

"Maybe *you* should run for class president," said Mrs. Sanchez.

"I wouldn't be any good as president," Julio said. "Lucas is really smart. He'd be great."

"You're smart, too," said Mrs. Sanchez. "You should have more confidence in yourself."

"You're just saying that because you're my mother," said Julio. He sat digesting chicken and digesting his mother's words, too. He wished he had the nerve to run for class president. "Anyway, I already told Lucas I would help him run."

"Tell him you changed your mind," said Mrs. Sanchez.

"He's my friend," Julio protested. "I can't change my mind because I told him I'd help him."

"If he's your friend, he'll understand," said Julio's mother.

Julio wished he had never mentioned the class election. In his heart, he knew he liked the idea of being president of his class. He wished he had the courage to run.

"I bet no one would even vote for me," he said.

"How can you know if you don't try?" asked Julio's grandmother in Spanish.

It was funny, Julio thought. Sometimes when they were speaking English, he was sure his grandmother didn't even know what they were talking about. Tonight he saw that she did understand.

"Mama's right," said Ramon. "What have you got to lose?"

"Just the election," joked Nelson.

"Maybe he won't lose. Maybe he'll win," said Ramon.

"When you are elected president, I'll cook a special dinner to celebrate," said Mrs. Sanchez. She seemed to think the matter was settled. All her son had to do was run and he would be elected.

His mother looked so excited that Julio was sorry that he was going to disappoint her. She didn't seem to realize that it wasn't so easy to become class president. She had never met Cricket or most of his other classmates. They'd *never* vote for him. They'd probably fall over laughing at the thought of it. Tomorrow he'd start campaigning for Lucas Cott.

★3★
A
GOOD LEADER

The next morning in Mr. Flores's class, everyone was kept busy discussing how he or she was going to spend a million dollars. Just before lunchtime, Cricket raised her hand. "Can't we vote for a class president today?" she asked. She was probably going to nag the teacher about it every day, thought Julio.

"What's the rush?" asked Mr. Flores. "This is only the second day of school. We have a whole year ahead of us."

"Don't remind me," Julio groaned under his

breath, but loudly enough for Lucas and others nearby to hear.

"You said we should wait to know each other better," Cricket pointed out. "But we already know each other."

"Yeah," several of the fifth graders chorused.

"It's true you know each other better than I know you," said Mr. Flores. "But since you've never voted for a class president before, you may not have thought about what qualities a president should have."

"It's got to be somebody that everyone likes," said Arthur.

"True," Mr. Flores said. "However, is an election just a popularity contest? Does the most popular person make the best president?"

"It's the most popular person who always wins an election," said Zoe.

"Yes. Nevertheless, a person should be popular for the right reasons," said Mr. Flores. "What other qualities should a good president have?"

No one answered. Even Cricket, who always had the right answers to even the hardest questions, didn't know what to say.

"What about leadership ability?" asked Mr. Flores.

"But the teacher is the leader," said Cricket.

"Of course," said Mr. Flores. "But the student you elect must have the *potential* to be a leader, even though the teacher is still in charge."

"Sometimes teachers are absent," Lucas pointed out.

"Yeah, but then we get a substitute," said Julio.

Just then the bell rang for lunch. "We'll have an election on the second Friday in September," said Mr. Flores. "I want you to think hard about the best candidate for the job. Look for a good leader, someone who is fair and who stands up for what he or she thinks is right. Think about someone who is concerned about the whole class and not just a few special friends."

Julio looked at Cricket. She was very smart and she spoke out a lot in class. Probably she would make an okay president, but he didn't think she thought about anyone except herself and a few of the girls who were her friends. Mr. Flores was right, Julio thought as the class headed down to the lunchroom. He wondered if he himself had what it took to be a good leader.

Lunch that day was another of Julio's favorites—hot diggity dog, a fancy name for a hot dog on a bun, with potato puffs, coleslaw, and oatmeal-raisin cookies.

Cricket looked around the table. "If you vote for me," she told everyone, "you *know* you'll get a *smart* president."

"Zoe is smart, too," said Sara Jane.

"I don't want to be president," said Zoe. "I'm voting for Cricket."

"Lucas is going to run for president," Julio announced.

"You are?" Cricket asked him.

"I might," said Lucas.

"I'm going to be his campaign manager," Julio said.

"Then he'll never win," said Cricket.

"Aren't you finished yet?" Lucas asked Julio. "Let's go out and play soccer. We're not having the election yet."

Julio licked the mustard off his fingers and gathered up his lunch tray. "I'm coming," he said. Soccer was a lot more important than the election.

Outside, the boys quickly formed teams. Some

days the girls played soccer, too. Or sometimes they jumped rope together. Julio was the best player and he was chosen captain of one team. Everyone wanted to be on Julio's team. At recess, Julio was a leader, but not in the classroom.

Arthur Lewis stood watching. He didn't move very quickly and he had never scored a goal in his life. He was surprised and grateful when Julio picked him for his team.

Julio kicked the ball and immediately scored a goal. "Yeaaa, Julio!" Zoe Mitchell called out

from the sidelines.

Julio heard a noise behind him. He turned and saw that Arthur Lewis had fallen down. The other kids kept on playing, running around Arthur as he slowly got up.

"Where are my glasses?" asked Arthur. Julio saw Arthur's glasses on the ground. Just then, the soccer ball landed on top of them, breaking the frame right in half. One of the lenses was cracked, too.

The soccer game stopped and everyone gathered around Arthur to see what had happened.

"They're not looking too good," said Julio, picking up the glasses and handing them to their owner.

"My new glasses! They cost a lot of money and they're supposed to be unbreakable." Arthur's eyes filled with tears. "My mother is going to have a fit."

"Crybaby. Crybaby," someone called out.

"He's not crying," said Julio. "His eyes are tearing because he's straining to see without his glasses."

Julio put his arm around Arthur's shoulders. "Don't worry," he said. "We'll all chip in and help you pay for them."

"Hey, no way," said one of the boys. "Just because he falls over his own feet doesn't mean we have to pay for his glasses."

"Who kicked the ball that landed on the glasses?" asked another boy.

"That doesn't matter," said Julio. "We were all playing, so we should all chip in. It's only fair."

"It's an awful lot of money," said Arthur. "I don't think you'll be able to pay for them."

"Don't worry," said Julio. "We'll figure out a

way." He stuck his hands into his pockets. He had a quarter and two pennies. He handed them to Arthur. "This is just for a start," he said. "Who else has some money?"

"I spent my allowance already," said Sara Jane Cushman. "Besides, the girls weren't even playing soccer today."

"That's not the point," said Julio. "Arthur's in our class and I think we should all help him out."

Lucas handed over a dime and two quarters. Even without his glasses on, Arthur could figure out that he had only eighty-seven cents. It wasn't even enough for the tiny screws on the frames.

The teacher who was supervising recess came over to see what was wrong. "Is anyone hurt?" she asked.

"Just his glasses," said Julio as the bell rang for the students to return to the building. Julio kept his arm around Arthur's shoulders as they went inside. "It's okay," he said. "We'll get the money. Tell your mother not to worry. It will just take a little more time."

"I hope it doesn't take too long. I can hardly see anything without my glasses," complained Arthur.

"I'll be your Seeing Eye boy," Julio said, and he guided Arthur right to his seat.

"Arthur broke his glasses," Cricket announced when they were all seated.

"Kevin Shea did it," said Sara Jane. "He kicked the soccer ball that landed on Arthur's glasses."

Everyone spoke at once, trying to explain the accident. Finally, Mr. Flores had the whole picture.

"We should all chip in and help pay for the new glasses," said Julio. "We could earn the money."

Mr. Flores looked at Julio. "That's a good idea," he said. "Any suggestions on how we could do it?"

"We could put on a play and charge admission," said Lucas.

"A project like that would take a long time," said Mr. Flores. "If we're going to pay for Arthur's glasses, we have to do something quickly."

"I know," said Cricket. "We could have a bake sale. My mother taught me how to make chocolate-chip cookies. If everyone baked one thing, we could have a big sale. We could do it tomorrow!"

"I can make cupcakes," said Sara Jane.

"My mother makes great peanut-butter cookies," said Lucas. "I bet she'd help me make some for the sale."

Soon everyone had suggestions for what they could bake. Julio had never baked anything in his life and he knew his mother would be too tired to start making cakes or cookies when she got home from work.

"What about you, Julio?" asked Cricket. She was making a list of what everyone could bring. "We already have cupcakes and two kinds of cookies. We can't have too many people making the same things."

Julio thought fast. "Brownies," he said. "With lots of nuts."

"Good," said Cricket, and she wrote that down on her list.

"Tomorrow seems too soon," said Mr. Flores as the students went on with their planning. "Let's have this sale on Friday. We'll put up signs around the school so everyone will know about it and then they'll bring a little extra money."

Arthur Lewis spent the rest of the afternoon in a haze. He couldn't concentrate because he was worrying about what his mother would say when she saw the glasses.

Julio Sanchez spent the rest of the afternoon in a daze. Somehow, he had to figure out how to make brownies between now and Friday. Brownies with lots of nuts! He must have been *nuts* himself.

★4★
SEEING EYE
BOY

After school, Julio walked home with Lucas until they reached the street where they always parted. "See you tomorrow," Lucas called after him.

Julio shifted his backpack and kept walking. He wondered what things besides chocolate you needed to make brownies. Milk? Eggs? Sugar? Nuts.

When he reached the next corner, he saw a boy sitting on the curb. It was Arthur Lewis.

"Hey, Arthur," Julio called out. "What are you doing here? Don't you take the bus?"

"I couldn't see the numbers on the buses without my glasses," Arthur explained, "so I didn't get on any bus at all. Now I'm probably going to get run over before I get home." Arthur sighed. "I don't want to go home, anyhow. My mother is going to be furious."

"Don't worry," Julio said. "Tell her that our class is going to raise the money for new glasses."

"You tell her," said Arthur. "She won't yell at you."

"Why would she yell at you? You didn't break the glasses on purpose."

"Oh, you know how mothers are. They always yell," said Arthur.

Julio thought Arthur was exaggerating. His own mother hardly ever yelled, but when she told him he had to do his homework before he could watch TV, he knew she meant business.

"Please come home with me," said Arthur. "You said you'd be my Seeing Eye boy."

"All right," Julio agreed. In all the years they'd known each other, Arthur had never invited Julio to his house before. "Let's get going. If you usually take the bus, it's going to be a long walk," said Julio.

"You're a real pal," said Arthur.

The two boys set off. As they walked, Arthur told Julio all the things he was going to buy with his imaginary million dollars. He had thought of some things that Julio hadn't, like a ticket to all the football games and a swimming pool in his backyard.

"I don't have a backyard, so I can't get a swimming pool," said Julio. "Can I come and swim in yours?"

"Sure," said Arthur. "You can come to the football games with me, too."

It sounded great until Julio remembered it was all pretend.

He felt in his pockets and found a pack of gum. "You want a piece?" he asked Arthur.

Arthur shook his head. "My mother doesn't let me chew gum," he said. "It's bad for your teeth."

Julio felt around in his mouth with his tongue. His teeth felt okay to him, so he kept on chewing.

"You know what, Julio?" said Arthur. "I think you'd be a good president for our class."

"Me?" said Julio, amazed. How did Arthur guess that he secretly wanted to be class president? "That's crazy," he said.

"No, it's not," said Arthur. "I'd vote for you. I bet a lot of kids would. You're always fair, and you're nice to everyone. You always pick me to be on your team even though I'm rotten at sports."

Julio thought about what Arthur had said. He wondered if anyone else would agree with Arthur—not including his mother, of course. She didn't count because she couldn't vote.

When they reached Arthur's house, Mrs. Lewis was standing outside. "Where were you?" she called to her son. "The bus went by half an hour ago. I was getting very worried."

"Mom, this is my friend Julio—" Arthur began, but Mrs. Lewis interrupted.

"Arthur, where are your glasses? Were you in an accident?"

"Arthur fell when we were playing soccer during recess," Julio explained. "He didn't get hurt but his glasses fell off and the soccer ball bounced on top of them."

"I just bought those glasses a week ago," said Mrs. Lewis, "and they're broken already."

"It was an accident," said Julio.

"Why were you playing soccer?" asked Mrs. Lewis. "Can't you find some quiet activity for after lunch? You could have gotten a stomachache, or broken your leg. I never played soccer once in my life. I don't see why you have to do something like that, either."

"Oh, Mom," said Arthur. "All the boys play soccer."

"Mrs. Lewis," said Julio, "Arthur didn't get a stomachache and he didn't break his leg. Our class is going to have a bake sale to earn money for a new pair of glasses. So you see, there's nothing to worry about."

Mrs. Lewis looked at Julio. "I don't think I heard your name," she said.

"I'm Julio. Julio Sanchez. I've been in Arthur's class a long time. I knew him even before he wore glasses."

"Well hello, Julio," said Mrs. Lewis. "It was nice of you to walk Arthur home. Come inside and I'll give you boys a snack."

Arthur's mother opened the door. There was a smell of something good cooking on the stove. Julio didn't recognize the smell but he liked it.

"Wash your hands," Mrs. Lewis told the boys.

Julio was about to say that his hands weren't dirty, but he thought better of it. He didn't want to upset Mrs. Lewis. Julio followed Arthur to the bathroom. It was all blue and white. Blue and white tiles, a blue basin, and even a blue toilet. The toilet paper was a blue and white pattern, the soap was blue, and the towels were blue-and-white striped. It was like a bathroom in a movie. He spit his piece of gum into the toilet and flushed it away.

Back in the kitchen, Mrs. Lewis had poured two glasses of milk and set out a plate of cookies. "Two each," she said. "I don't want to spoil your suppers."

Julio bit into one of the cookies, a soft oatmeal cookie with raisins in it. It was a hundred times better than the one he had eaten at school.

"These are great," Julio told Mrs. Lewis. "Maybe you could make some for the bake sale."

"When is this sale?" asked Mrs. Lewis.

"Friday," said Arthur. "I can wear my old glasses until then."

"And no soccer playing," said Mrs. Lewis.

Arthur nodded.

When they finished their snack, Arthur led the

way to his bedroom. He had a big room lined with shelves that were filled with games and toys.

Arthur didn't really need a million dollars, Julio thought. He had a lot of neat stuff already.

"Look at this," said Arthur, showing Julio an old kitchen clock. The hands on the clock said 1:15. Julio didn't have a watch, but he knew it had to be after four.

"It's got the wrong time," said Julio.

"Look some more," said Arthur.

"The second hand is moving *backward!*" said Julio in amazement.

"Right," said Arthur. "Isn't it neat? It got broken and now it runs the wrong way. My mother was going to throw it out but I asked her to let me keep it. Every other clock in the world goes in a different direction from mine."

"Yours runs counterclockwise," said Julio.

"Right," said Arthur. "Sometimes I like things that are different."

Julio looked around at Arthur's bedroom. The bedspread matched the curtains. There was a carpet on the floor and many toys, but Arthur's favorite thing was the broken clock. Julio's grandmother always said that it took all kinds of people to make up the world. She said it in Spanish, but it was true in English, too.

Julio stayed at Arthur's until the counterclockwise clock said it was quarter to one. Then he walked home slowly. Arthur sure was a funny kid. That's probably why he thought Julio should run for president.

★5★
A
GOOEY MESS

When Julio got home, Nelson was in the kitchen cutting up vegetables for dinner.

"Can you make brownies?" Julio asked him. "I have to make some for a bake sale at school on Friday, but I don't know how."

Nelson shrugged his shoulders. "You can buy brownie mix at the supermarket," he suggested. "Everything you need will be in the box and it will have directions to show you what to do."

"Great!" shouted Julio with relief. Making brownies wouldn't be so hard if all the ingredients came together in one box. Julio was even happier when he convinced Nelson to lend him five dollars so he could go shopping to get the brownie mix right away.

Julio had given his own money to Arthur, and even if he hadn't, he doubted that twenty-seven cents would have gone very far toward his purchase.

"I'll pay you back," Julio promised Nelson.

"Sure," said Nelson, grinning. "Put it in the glove compartment of that car you're going to buy me with your million dollars."

At the supermarket, Julio found a whole row of shelves filled with mixes to make cakes, cookies, gingerbread, and a hundred other desserts. The pictures on the boxes looked delicious. Julio took three different boxes of brownie mix off the shelves and studied them carefully. Finally, he picked the box that had the best picture, even though it cost twenty cents more than the others. He decided to buy two boxes so he could make twice as many brownies.

After supper, Julio showed his mother the packages of brownie mix. "Can you help me make this?" he asked.

Mrs. Sanchez read the instructions on one of the boxes. "It's easy," she said. "You just add a couple of things to the mix and bake it in the oven."

"Can we do it now?" asked Julio. "I have to take them to school on Friday."

"This is only Tuesday," said Mrs. Sanchez. "If we do it now, the brownies will be stale by Friday."

"They will be *gone* by Friday," Julio's grandmother said in Spanish.

She was probably right, thought Julio. It would be awful if he baked the brownies and they were all eaten before he got them to school.

"Okay. Thursday night," said Julio. "We'll make the brownies then."

Wednesday's school lunch was tacos with cheese and lettuce, buttered corn, and baked beans. The Thursday menu featured oven-fried chicken, mashed potatoes, and green beans. It was heaven after all those peanut-butter sandwiches. Everyone was eagerly awaiting the bake sale. Cricket and Zoe had made big colorful signs at home and had brought them to school to advertise the event. In fact, Cricket was so involved

with the bake sale that she stopped tal.
the class election. Still, she did bring a
tiny chocolate bars in her lunch, and she
one to every kid in the class. Julio was sure it w
a bribe to get them to vote for her for class president.

Arthur Lewis came to school wearing his old
glasses. Although his parents had been upset that
his glasses were broken on the second day of
school, he felt pretty important, too. After all, if
he hadn't broken his glasses, there wouldn't be
a class bake sale.

After supper on Thursday evening, Julio took
his two boxes of brownie mix from the kitchen
cabinet. "Can you help me?" he asked his
mother.

Mrs. Sanchez had just sat down on the living
room sofa. "Oh, Julio." She sighed. "I have an
awful headache tonight. Please ask your brother
to help you. If you get stuck, let me know."

Ramon was taking a class that evening, but
Nelson was glad to be released from his homework. "I like your homework much better than
mine," said Nelson as he read the directions on
the box.

Julio opened one of the packages of brownie mix. Inside was just some brown powder. Julio hoped he wasn't going to be cheated by the company that sold this stuff.

"It sure doesn't look like any brownies I ever saw," he said.

"Of course not. It needs two eggs and water and cooking oil added to it," said Nelson.

Julio went to the refrigerator. "There're two packages, so we need four eggs."

Nelson found a large bowl in the cupboard and the boys broke the eggs into it. Then they emptied the two boxes into the bowl. Julio began to mix the eggs and powder together while Nelson filled a measuring cup with water and then added the oil.

Julio and Nelson took turns stirring the gooey mixture. Julio stuck his finger in the bowl for a taste.

"Hey," he said suddenly. "Where are the nuts?"

"Why do you need nuts?" asked Nelson.

Julio looked inside the empty boxes. "I like brownies with nuts. I promised that there would be nuts in my brownies."

"So go get some. It's not too late," said Nelson. He gave Julio two dollars more, and Julio rushed off to the supermarket. Twenty minutes later, he returned home with a cellophane bag filled with walnuts.

"Why did you get nuts with shells?" asked Nelson.

"All nuts have shells," said Julio. "That's how they grow. We learned that back in first grade."

"You dumb kid," said Nelson. "You can buy them already shelled. Now we have to crack them open." He looked around for something heavy to use.

Julio took a heavy pot from the cupboard. Nelson took another one. They put the nuts on the floor and began to pound them. "I didn't know squirrels had to work so hard," Nelson complained.

Mrs. Sanchez came into the kitchen to investigate. "This is not good medicine for a headache," she chided her sons.

Someone was banging at the front door. It was like an echo of the banging in the kitchen. Julio went to check. He looked through the peephole and saw their downstairs neighbor, Mr. Findlay.

"Is everything okay?" the old man asked when Julio opened the door.

"Sure," said Julio. "Everything's fine."

"I heard an awful banging, and I thought something was the matter."

Julio's mother went to the door. She invited their neighbor in for a cup of tea.

Finally, after half an hour of hitting nuts and fingers, all the walnut shells were cracked and there was a whole pile of broken walnut pieces. Nelson gathered them up and threw them into the bowl of brownie batter. "At last we're done," he said. "This is as hard as my algebra homework. Maybe harder."

"These aren't brownies yet," protested Julio.

"Of course not. We have to bake them."

The box said to heat the oven to 350 degrees.

Julio poured the gooey chocolaty mess into a big pan. Nelson stuck the pan inside the oven.

"It's eight-fifteen," said Nelson. "Watch the clock and call me when it's quarter to nine. I'm going to do some relaxing algebra in the meantime."

Julio sat down at the kitchen table. He looked at the clock. Only twenty-nine more minutes to go. He ran his finger along the inside of the bowl and licked the batter off his finger. Then he picked up one of the empty boxes of brownie mix and read the directions again.

They had done everything just right. Julio noticed that in very tiny print it said, "Optional: Nuts may be added." The picture on the box showed nuts sticking out of the brownies. It didn't seem very honest if the nuts weren't in the box.

Julio turned back to the directions. The box said, "Bake for thirty minutes in a greased baking pan."

"Nelson!" he shouted. He ran into the bedroom where Nelson was doing his homework and listening to loud rock music at the same time. "Did we grease the baking pan?"

Nelson threw down his pencil and rushed into the living room to tell his mother. Julio followed. "Did we do something wrong?" he asked.

Mrs. Sanchez ran into the kitchen and grabbed a pot holder. She pulled the pan of brownies from the oven. They were still a gooey mess. "Give me the bowl," she said to Julio.

Julio grabbed the bowl that he had put in the sink, and Mrs. Sanchez tipped the pan and poured the hot batter back into the bowl. Julio's grandmother and Mr. Findlay came into the kitchen to see what was going on.

"If you don't grease the pan, the brownies will stick to it," Mrs. Sanchez explained.

When the batter was back in the bowl, Mrs. Sanchez put the pan in the sink and washed it out.

"What are you doing?" Julio asked anxiously. It looked as if they were working backward. Soon they would remove the nuts from the brownies and put them back into the walnut shells.

"Get me the margarine from the refrigerator," said Mrs. Sanchez.

Julio put a half stick of margarine on the counter. His mother handed the baking pan to Nelson, who dried it quickly with the dish towel. Mrs. Sanchez cut off a piece of margarine and, with a bit of paper towel, she rubbed it all over the bottom of the pan. "This is greasing the pan," she explained.

"It's not something they teach you at school," said Nelson.

"Will the brownies still turn out okay?" asked Julio.

"They smell good to me," said Mr. Findlay.

Nelson poured the batter back into the pan and slid it into the oven. Julio looked at the clock. It was quarter to nine.

By nine o'clock, the whole apartment began to smell like chocolate brownies. Promptly at 9:15, Nelson went and opened the oven. He took out the pan. The brownies looked good and they smelled even better. Julio's mother and grandmother and Mr. Findlay came back to the kitchen.

Julio hoped that they all wouldn't want to taste his brownies. There might be none left for selling at school. But when the brownies cooled and Nelson helped him cut them into small squares, they only nibbled at the tiny crumbs that fell off.

"It really worked," said Julio as he helped himself to one of the larger crumbs. "I really made brownies!"

"*You* made brownies," said Nelson, giving him a nudge. "What about me?"

"We made brownies," said Julio, correcting himself. "Aren't you glad I let you help me with my homework?"

★6★
A VERY
SMART COOKIE

Friday of the first week of school was the bake sale. Everyone in Julio's class went to school carrying bags and boxes of home-baked goodies. The packages were piled up on a large table in Mr. Flores's classroom. All morning, during arithmetic and social studies, the scent of chocolate, peanuts, and cinnamon drifted through the room. Julio kept looking up to check that his box of brownies was still there.

Mr. Flores brought something to school that day, too. It was a guitar.

"Can you play that?" asked Arthur Lewis in amazement.

Mr. Flores nodded his head.

When they were small kids, their kindergarten teacher had played little melodies on a piano in the classroom, but since those days so long ago, the only person who performed any music was Mrs. Guinn, the special music teacher who came to the school two days a week. She taught the children new songs and music appreciation, but they never had any music unless they were in the music room.

"Will you play something for us?" asked Zoe.

"This afternoon," said Mr. Flores. "We are going to have folksinging on Friday afternoons."

Julio didn't know what folksinging was but it sounded a lot better than arithmetic or social studies. Maybe Mr. Flores knew some rock songs.

Lunch on Friday was a fish burger in a bun, with coleslaw and orange slices.

"Gross!" said Arthur. He always brought his lunch from home.

Julio took a bite of his fish burger, pretended to gag, and let his body go limp at the table. "They got me this time," he moaned. He liked fish burgers, but he didn't want to let anyone know.

After lunch, Cricket and Zoe put up a sign outside the classroom. Cricket made up the name "The Very Smart Cookie" because there was a bakery called "The Smart Cookie" near the school. They already had hung signs all around the school building. A few teachers had arranged with Mr. Flores that they would take their classes to the sale. Julio thought they would make a lot of money—enough to pay for Arthur's new glasses.

Promptly at 1:30, Mrs. Hockaday arrived with her third-grade class. Julio thought the kids looked like little babies. He couldn't believe that he had been that small when he was in third grade. Arthur, Sara Jane, and Zoe were taking their turn acting as salespeople.

"Show them my brownies," Julio called out.

"Julio," said Mrs. Hockaday, smiling at her former student, "do you still call out in class? I guess you haven't changed much at all."

Julio grinned. "I'm still me," he agreed, "but this is the first time I ever made brownies."

Mrs. Hockaday paid the fifteen-cent price and

took a bite of one of Julio's brownies. "This is delicious, Julio," she said.

After that, all the third graders wanted to buy Julio's brownies.

"I guess Mrs. Hockaday just gave you a celebrity endorsement," Lucas said to Julio. "It's the same as why you want to buy sneakers like those of a famous basketball player in a TV commercial."

The third graders were buying Julio's brownies so fast, he was sorry that he hadn't made more. By the time he had a turn to be a salesperson, there wouldn't be any left.

Mr. Flores opened his guitar case and began strumming.

"Play a song we all know," said Julio.

Mr. Flores played "She'll be coming 'round the mountain," and even the third graders, with their mouths full of brownies, sang along, too.

When Mrs. Hockaday's class left, Cricket, Lucas, and Anne Crosby took over the cookie sales. Mr. Flores kept strumming his guitar. Julio hoped there would be something left to sell when it was his turn.

"We already made three dollars and seventy-five cents," said Cricket, counting the coins in the money box.

Other classes came and went. A few mothers came to the sale, too. Lucas was back in his seat and Julio was selling cookies when Lucas's mother arrived with Lucas's little brothers.

"Uh-oh, here comes trouble," Julio muttered when he saw the almost-four-year-old twins. Marcus and Marius were famous for their mischief.

"Hi, Julio," called out either Marcus or Marius. Even though he had known them all their lives, Julio had never figured out a way to tell the twins apart.

Marcus or Marius grabbed a chocolate-chip cookie from the display on the table.

"Hey, that costs ten cents," said Julio. Either Marcus or Marius stuffed the cookie into his mouth, and the other twin grabbed a cookie, too.

"Mrs. Cott, you owe us twenty cents," called Julio. Then, either Marcus or Marius grabbed another cookie.

"Make that thirty cents," said Julio.

Lucas got out of his seat. The students had been told that only the salespeople were to leave

their seats during the bake sale. But the arrival of his twin brothers had to be a reason to break the rule. There was no way his mother could control both of his brothers at the same time— especially when they were facing a tableful of cookies and cakes.

"Hey Lucas, let them take all they want," Julio protested. "That's how we'll make a lot of money."

Mrs. Cott held out a dollar bill. "I will take seven more cookies, if you have a bag to put them in. Then we're going home," she said firmly.

Luckily, Cricket had thought of everything, including bags. Julio put seven cookies in a bag and put the dollar bill into the money box. By now, there were a number of bills and loads of change. He hoped there would be enough for Arthur's glasses.

Mr. Flores nodded to the next group of sales-people. Julio stepped out from behind the table.

"I'm thirsty," said either Marcus or Marius.

Too bad we're not selling containers of milk, Julio thought. That was one thing Cricket hadn't thought of.

"You can have a drink when we get home," Mrs. Cott said to either Marcus or Marius.

"I want a drink now," said either Marcus or Marius.

"I could take them to the fountain," offered Julio. He turned to Mr. Flores, who nodded that he could leave the room.

Julio took each twin by the hand. Their hands were sticky from the cookies, but walking with them made him feel very grown-up. He wondered if Nelson and Ramon had felt that way walking with him when he was little.

When they reached the fountain, Julio let go of their hands. He realized that the boys were too short to reach the fountain at this end of the hallway. There was a lower fountain outside of the kindergarten room. He should have thought of taking them there.

"Let me help you," he said to either Marcus or Marius. He lifted him up so his mouth could reach the spigot where the water came out. "Push the button," Julio said.

Either Marcus or Marius pushed it, and the water came out. The little boy made a loud slurping sound as he drank. Julio remembered that he had done the same thing in kindergarten. Slurping was a big deal with little kids.

"Now me, now me," said the other twin.

Julio put either Marcus or Marius down and picked up either Marcus or Marius. They felt exactly the same weight, their voices were the same, and they looked identical. Poor Lucas, he thought as he held one of his friend's brothers up to the fountain. How can he ever know to whom he is talking?

"I have to make peepee," said the twin whom Julio wasn't holding.

The other twin stopped slurping. "Me, too," he said.

Julio put down either Marcus or Marius. "I'll take you to the boys' room," he told them, and he quickly led the way. He didn't want any accidents right there in the hallway.

In the bathroom, Julio helped one of the twins unzip his pants and then he waited. Nothing happened.

"I thought you had to go to the toilet," Julio said.

"I don't have to go anymore," said either Marcus or Marius.

"What about you?" Julio said, turning to look for the other twin. While Julio's back was turned, the little boy had climbed up onto the washbasin and filled his hands with liquid soap from the dispenser. He rubbed the liquid soap into his hair.

"Stop that," said Julio. "I thought you had to go to the toilet."

"Not now," said either Marcus or Marius. "I am having a shampoo." By now, there was quite a lather of soapsuds in his hair.

"I want one, too," said the other twin.

"No," said Julio. "School is not a place for shampoos. Nobody comes to school for a shampoo."

The twin without soapsuds in his hair began to cry in protest.

"You have to let me rinse the soap off," Julio said to the other twin. He turned on the water tap. Only the cold one worked.

"You got soap in my eyes," cried the little boy as Julio splashed cold water onto his head. Now both twins were crying.

The door to the boys' bathroom opened and

Lucas came in. "What's going on?" he asked over the sound of both twins crying.

"Man, your mother must be strong to be able to put up with both of these kids at once," said Julio. "I took them for a drink and then they said they wanted to go to the toilet and then when I wasn't looking, this one started to give himself a shampoo. They've knocked me out."

"Shampoo? Marius, you hate shampoos," said Lucas, grabbing some paper towels to help dry his brother's head.

"I like shampoos at school," said Marius.

"How can you even tell who he is?" asked Julio.

"If you live with them every day, then you know," said Lucas simply.

Julio and Lucas took the two little boys back to the classroom. Mrs. Cott was talking to Cricket Kaufman's mother. Cricket's little sister, Monica, was standing nearby looking like a little angel. She would probably never grab a cookie or give herself a shampoo in the school bathroom.

Julio explained why one twin had wet hair. He was afraid Mrs. Cott would be angry at him. He probably didn't have much leadership ability if he couldn't even lead two little boys to the water fountain.

"Don't worry, Julio. You were a very smart cookie to keep up with these two," said Mrs. Cott.

She pulled up the hood on the sweat shirt the little boy was wearing so his head would be warm on the way home. Then she picked up her bag of cookies and waved good-bye to Mr. Flores and the class.

Julio sat down in his seat, exhausted. A moment later, Arthur Lewis's mother arrived. She had a big smile on her face. In a voice loud enough for everyone in the class to hear, she told Mr. Flores that because Arthur's glasses broke within two weeks of his getting them, they were going to be replaced for free.

"Then we didn't need to have this bake sale at all," said Cricket after Mrs. Lewis had left.

Everyone began to speak at once.

Mr. Flores played a loud chord on his guitar and the class quieted down.

"The sale was fun, wasn't it?" he asked them.

Everyone nodded in agreement.

"What will we do with the money now?" asked Cricket.

"I'm sure we can think of a good way to spend it before the year is out," said Mr. Flores.

"We could have a party," suggested Sara Jane.

"Or give it to charity," said Zoe.

"There are a lot of possibilities. We don't have to make a decision today," said Mr. Flores.

By the time the bell rang for dismissal, there was not one cookie or piece of cake or brownie left to be sold. The class had made seventeen dollars and forty cents, which Mr. Flores would hold for them.

"Don't spend it all over the weekend," said Julio. He was only kidding. He knew Mr. Flores wouldn't do that.

"You can trust me," Mr. Flores promised, holding out his hand to Julio.

Julio shook the extended hand. Fifth grade was turning out to be his best year yet.

★7★
JULIO
IN THE
LION'S DEN

On Monday, Arthur came to school with new glasses. Cricket came to class with a big poster that said, VOTE FOR CRICKET, THAT'S THE TICKET.

The election was going to be held on Friday. That meant there were only four days more to get ready. In the meantime, they learned about how to make a nomination and how to second it. It was going to be a really serious election.

At lunch, Cricket took out a bag of miniature chocolate bars and gave them out to her classmates. Julio took his and ate it. But it didn't mean he was going to vote for Cricket. He wondered if there was anything Lucas could give out that was better than chocolate. Nothing was better than chocolate!

"If you're going to run against Cricket, we've got to get to work," Julio told Lucas on their way home. Julio wasn't very good at making posters, as Cricket and Zoe were, but he was determined to help his friend.

The next morning, a new poster appeared in Mr. Flores's classroom. It said, DON'T BUG ME. VOTE FOR LUCAS COTT. Julio had made it.

Before lunch, Mr. Flores read an announcement from the principal. "From now on, there is to be no more soccer playing in the school yard at lunchtime."

"No more soccer playing?" Julio called out. "Why not?"

Mr. Flores looked at Julio. "If you give me a moment, I'll explain. Mr. Herbertson is concerned about accidents. Last week, Arthur broke his glasses. Another time, someone might be injured more seriously."

Julio was about to call out again, but he remembered just in time and raised his hand.

"Yes, Julio," said Mr. Flores.

"It's not fair to make us stop playing soccer just because someone *might* get hurt. Someone might fall down walking to school, but we still have to come to school every day."

Julio didn't mean to be funny, but everyone started to laugh. Even Mr. Flores smiled.

"There must be other activities to keep you fellows busy at lunchtime," he said. "Is soccer the only thing you can do?"

Lucas raised his hand. "I don't like jumping rope," he said when the teacher called on him.

All the girls giggled at that.

"You could play jacks," suggested Cricket. Everyone knew it wasn't a serious possibility, though.

"Couldn't we tell Mr. Herbertson that we want to play soccer?" asked Julio.

"You could make an appointment to speak to him, if you'd like," said Mr. Flores. "He might change his decision if you convince him that you are right."

"Lucas and I will talk to him," said Julio. "Right, Lucas?"

"Uh, sure," said Lucas, but he didn't look too sure.

The principal, Mr. Herbertson, spoke in a loud voice and had eyes that seemed to bore right into your head when he looked at you. Julio had been a little bit afraid of Mr. Herbertson since the very first day of kindergarten. Why had he offered to go to his office and talk to him?

Mr. Flores sent Julio and Lucas down to the principal's office with a note, but the principal was out of the office at a meeting.

"You can talk to him at one o'clock," the secretary said.

At lunch, Cricket had more chocolate bars. This time, she had pasted labels on them and printed in tiny letters, *Cricket is the ticket.* She must be spending her whole allowance on the campaign, Julio thought.

After a few more days of free chocolate bars, everyone in the class would be voting for Cricket.

At recess, the girls were jumping rope. You could fall jumping rope, too, Julio thought.

Back in the classroom, Julio wished he could think up some good arguments to tell the principal. He looked over at Lucas. Lucas didn't look very good. Maybe he was coming down with the flu.

Just before one o'clock, Julio had a great idea. Cricket was always saying she wanted to be a lawyer. She always knew what to say in class. Julio figured she'd know just what to do in the principal's office, too. He raised his hand.

"Mr. Flores, can Cricket go down to Mr. Herbertson's office with Lucas and me? She's running for president, so she should stick up for our class."

"Me?" Cricket said. "I don't care if we can't play soccer."

"Of course," teased Lucas. "You couldn't kick a ball if it was glued to your foot."

"Cricket," said Mr. Flores, "even if you don't want to play soccer, others in the class do. If you are elected, you will be president of the whole class, not just the girls. I think going to the meeting with Mr. Herbertson will be a good opportunity for you to represent the class."

So that was why at one o'clock Julio, Lucas, and Cricket Kaufman went downstairs to the principal's office.

Mr. Herbertson gestured for them to sit in the chairs facing his desk. Cricket looked as pale as Lucas. Maybe she, too, was coming down with the flu.

Julio waited for the future first woman President of the United States to say something, but Cricket didn't say a word. Neither did Lucas. Julio didn't know what to do. They couldn't just sit here and say nothing.

Julio took a deep breath. If Cricket or Lucas wasn't going to talk, he would have to do it. Julio started right in.

"We came to tell you that it isn't fair that no one can play soccer at recess just because Arthur Lewis broke his eyeglasses. Anybody can have an accident. He could have tripped and broken them getting on the school bus." Julio was amazed that so many words had managed to get out of his mouth. No one else said anything, so he went on. "Besides, a girl could fall jumping rope," said Julio. "But you didn't say that they had to stop jumping rope."

"I hadn't thought of that," said Mr. Herbertson.

Cricket looked alarmed. "Can't we jump rope anymore?" she asked.

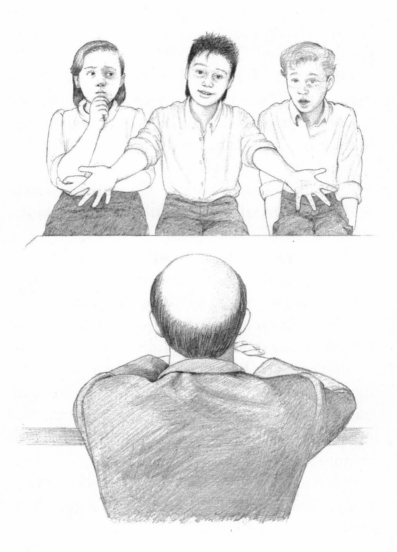

"I didn't mean that you should make the girls stop jumping rope," Julio went on quickly. He stopped to think of a better example. "Your chair could break while you're sitting on it, Mr. Herbertson," he said.

Mr. Herbertson adjusted himself in his chair. "I certainly hope not," he said, smiling. "What is your name, young man?"

"Julio. Julio Sanchez." He pronounced it in the Spanish way with the *J* having an *H* sound.

"You have a couple of brothers who also attended this school, Julio, don't you?" asked the principal. "Nice fellows. I remember them both."

Julio smiled. He didn't know why he had always been afraid of the principal. He was just like any other person.

"Julio," Mr. Herbertson went on, "you've got a good head on your shoulders, just like your brothers. You made some very good points this afternoon. I think I can arrange things so that there will be more teachers supervising the yard during recess. Then you fellows can play soccer again tomorrow." He turned to Cricket. "You can jump rope if you'd rather do that," he said.

Cricket smiled. She didn't look so pale anymore.

Julio and Lucas and Cricket returned to Mr. Flores's classroom. "It's all arranged," said Cricket as soon as they walked in the door.

The class burst into cheers.

"Good work," said Mr. Flores.

Julio was proud that he had stood up to Mr. Herbertson. However, it wasn't fair that Cricket made it seem as if she had done all the work. She had hardly done a thing. For that matter, Lucas hadn't said anything, either. For a moment, Julio wished he hadn't offered to be Lucas's campaign manager. He wished he was the one running for class president. He knew he could be a good leader.

★ 8 ★
CLASS
PRESIDENT

There was bad news on election day. Chris Willard was absent. Since there were twelve girls and twelve boys in Mr. Flores's class, it meant there were more girls than boys to vote in the election. If all the girls voted for Cricket and all the boys voted for Lucas, there would be a tie. Since one boy was absent, Lucas could be in big trouble. Julio hoped it didn't mean that Lucas had lost the election before they even voted.

Then Mr. Flores told the class that the Parent–Teacher Association was going to be holding a book fair in a few weeks. With more than seventeen dollars from the bake sale, the class could buy a good supply of paperbacks for a special classroom library. Cricket seemed to think it was a great idea, but Julio didn't think it was so hot. After all, there was a school library up one flight of stairs. Why did they need extra books, especially books the students had to pay for out of their *own* money?

Julio thought that the class should vote on the way the money was spent. Before he had a chance to say anything, it was time for lunch.

Lunch was chicken nuggets, whipped potatoes, string beans, and Jell-O squares. Cricket and Zoe didn't even touch their lunches. Julio knew they were talking about the election. Julio clapped Lucas on the back. "You're going to win, pal," he said. "I just know it." He really wasn't so sure, but he felt it was his job to give his candidate confidence. After all, he had convinced Lucas to run for class president in the first place.

Lucas shrugged, trying to act cool. "Maybe yes, maybe no," he said. But Julio could see that he was too excited to eat much lunch, either.

Julio polished off his friend's tuna-fish sandwich and his orange. "I need to keep up my strength to vote for you," he told Lucas.

Cricket had more chocolate bars. "Are you going to vote for me?" she asked everyone.

"Maybe yes, maybe no," said Julio, taking his bar.

When they returned from lunch, Mr. Flores called the class to order. It was time for the election to begin. Mr. Flores reminded them about *Robert's Rules of Order*, which was the way school board and other important meetings were conducted.

"You may nominate anyone you choose," he said, "even if your candidate doesn't have a poster up on the wall. Then you can make a speech in favor of your candidate and try to convince your classmates."

Uh-oh, thought Julio. He was ready to nominate Lucas but he didn't know if he would be able to make a speech. He wasn't good with words, as Cricket and Lucas were.

Zoe Mitchell raised her hand. "I nominate Cricket Kaufman," she said. No surprise there.

Julio wondered if Zoe had wanted to run herself.

"Does anyone second the nomination?" Mr. Flores asked.

Julio thought the class election sounded like a TV program, not the way people talked in real life.

Sara Jane seconded the nomination, and Mr. Flores wrote Cricket's name on the chalkboard.

"Are there any other nominations?" he asked.

Sara Jane raised her hand again.

"Do you have a question, Sara Jane?" asked Mr. Flores.

"Now I want to nominate Zoe Mitchell."

"You can't nominate someone when you have already seconded the nomination of someone else," Mr. Flores explained. "That's the way parliamentary procedure works."

Cricket looked relieved. She hadn't been expecting any competition from Zoe.

Julio raised his hand. "I nominate Lucas Cott," he said.

"Does anyone second the nomination?"

"Can I second myself?" asked Lucas.

"I'll second the nomination," said Anne Crosby from the back of the classroom.

"*Ooooh*," giggled one of the girls. "Anne likes Lucas."

"There is no rule that girls can nominate only girls and boys nominate boys," said Mr. Flores. He wrote Lucas's name on the board. "Are there any other nominations?" he asked.

Arthur Lewis raised his hand. "I want to nominate Julio Sanchez," he said.

"Julio?" Sara Jane giggled. "He's just a big goof-off."

"Just a minute," said Mr. Flores sharply. "You are quite out of order, Sara Jane. Does anyone wish to second the nomination?"

Julio couldn't believe that Arthur had nominated him. Even though Arthur had said that Julio should run for president, Julio hadn't thought he would come right out and say it in front of everyone.

Cricket raised her hand. "Julio can't run for president," she said. "He was born in Puerto Rico. He isn't an American citizen. You have to be an American citizen to be elected President. We learned that last year in social studies."

"Yeah," Lucas called out. "You also have to

be thirty-five years old. You must have been left back a lot of times, Cricket."

"Hold on," said Mr. Flores. "Are we electing a President of the United States here, or are we electing a president of this fifth-grade class?"

Cricket looked embarrassed. It wasn't often she was wrong about anything.

Julio stood up without even raising his hand. He didn't care if he was elected president or not, but there was one thing he had to make clear. "I am so an American citizen," he said. "All Puerto Ricans are Americans!"

Julio sat down, and Arthur raised his hand again. Julio figured he was going to say he had changed his mind and didn't want to nominate him after all.

"Arthur?" called Mr. Flores.

Arthur stood up. "It doesn't matter where Julio was born," he said. "He'd make a very good class president. He's fair, and he's always doing nice things for people. When I broke my glasses, he was the one who thought of going to Mr. Herbertson so that we could still play soccer at recess. That shows he would make a good president."

"But Julio is not one of the top students like Zoe or Lucas or me," Cricket said.

"He is tops," said Arthur. "He's tops in my book."

Julio felt his ears getting hot with embarrassment. He had never heard Arthur say so much in all the years that he had known him.

"Thank you, Arthur," said Mr. Flores. "That was a very good speech. We still need someone to second the nomination. Do I hear a second?"

Lucas raised his hand.

"I second the nomination of Julio Sanchez," he said.

Mr. Flores turned to write Julio's name on the board. Lucas was still raising his hand.

Mr. Flores turned from the board and called on Lucas again.

"Do you wish to make a campaign speech?" he asked Lucas.

"Yes. I'm going to vote for Julio, and I think everyone else should, too."

"Aren't you even going to vote for yourself?" asked Cricket.

"No," said Lucas. "I want to take my name off the board. Julio is a good leader, like Arthur said. When we went to see Mr. Herbertson, Cricket and I were scared stiff, but Julio just stepped in and did all the talking."

"Are you asking to withdraw your name from nomination, Lucas?" asked Mr. Flores.

"Yes, I am. Everyone who was going to vote for me should vote for Julio."

Julio sat in his seat without moving. He couldn't say a word. He could hardly breathe.

"Are there any other nominations?" asked Mr. Flores.

Zoe raised her hand. "I move that the nominations be closed."

"I second it," said Lucas.

Then Mr. Flores asked the two candidates if they wanted to say anything to the class.

Cricket stood up. "As you all know," she said, "I'm going to run for President of the United States some day. Being class president will be good practice for me. Besides, I know I will do a much, much better job than Julio." Cricket sat down.

Julio stood. "I might vote for Cricket when she runs for President of the United States," he said. "But right now, I hope you will all vote for me.

I think our class should make decisions together, like how we should spend the money that we earned at the bake sale. We should spend the money in a way that everyone likes. Not just the teacher." Julio stopped and looked at Mr. Flores. "That's how I feel," he said.

"If I'm president," said Cricket, "I think the money should go to the Humane Society."

"*You* shouldn't tell us what to do with the money, either," said Julio. "It should be a class decision. We all helped to earn it."

"Julio has made a good point," said Mr. Flores. "I guess we can vote on that in the future."

Mr. Flores passed out the ballots. Julio was sure he knew the results even before the votes were counted. With one boy absent, Cricket would win, twelve to eleven.

Julio was right, and he was wrong. All the boys voted for him, but so did some of the girls. When the votes were counted, there were fourteen for Julio Sanchez and nine for Cricket Kaufman. Julio Sanchez was elected president of his fifth-grade class.

"I think you have made a good choice," said

Mr. Flores. "And I know that Cricket will be a very fine vice-president."

Julio beamed. Suddenly he was filled with all sorts of plans for his class.

Mr. Flores took out his guitar. As he had said, they were going to end each week with some singing. Julio thought he had never felt so much like singing in all his life. However, even as he joined the class in the words to the song, he wished it was already time to go home. He could hardly wait to tell his family the news. Wait till he told them who was the fifth-grade class president. Julio, that's who!

At three o'clock, he ran all the way home.